WONDER BOOKS®

Police Officers

A Level Three Reader

By Charnan Simon

Content Adviser: Bryce Kolpack,
Police Executive Research Forum, Washington, D.C.

Published by The Child's World®
P.O. Box 326
Chanhassen, MN 55317-0326
800-599-READ
www.childsworld.com

Photo Credits
© Adamsmith Productions/CORBIS: 6
© Bettmann/CORBIS: 18
© Douglas Kirkland/CORBIS: 5
© Jeff Hunter/ImageBank: cover
© Paul Hardy/CORBIS: 17
© Paul A. Souders/CORBIS: 9
© PhotoMondo/Taxi: 10
© Reuters NewMedia Inc./CORBIS: 29
© Rich Meyer/CORBIS: 3
© Ronnie Kaufman/CORBIS: 13
© Royalty-Free/CORBIS: 14, 22, 25
© Tim Wright/CORBIS: 21
© Tom Nebbia/CORBIS: 26

Editorial Directions, Inc.: E. Russell Primm and Emily J. Dolbear, Editors;
Alice K. Flanagan, Photo Researcher

The Child's World®: Mary Berendes, Publishing Director

Library of Congress Cataloging-in-Publication Data
Simon, Charnan.
Police officers / by Charnan Simon.
p. cm. — (Wonder books)
"A Level Three Reader."
Summary: A simple look at police officers and the many different kinds of work
that they do to keep their communities safe.
Includes bibliographical references and index.
ISBN 1-56766-476-8 (lib. bdg. : alk. paper)
1. Police—Juvenile literature. [1. Police. 2. Occupations.] I. Title. II. Series: Wonder books (Chanhassen, Minn.)
HV7922 .S56 2003
363.2—dc21 2002151412

Has a police officer ever helped you? A police officer's job is to protect and serve.

Police officers take care of the people in their community. They make sure people follow the law. They protect people from **criminals**. They work with the people in their community to help keep everyone safe.

This police officer is writing a ticket to a speeding driver.

20

METROPOLITAN
POLICE
HUGHES

Both men and women are police officers. All police officers are strong, smart, and brave. Their job is to solve problems and help people in trouble. Sometimes it can be a dangerous job.

← Police officers must be ready to help at all times.

People who want to become police officers go to a special school called a police **academy**. Today, these people go to college first. At the academy, they learn how to protect themselves. They study laws. They practice working with other officers so they can help each other.

These students are in training at a police academy. →

944
944
TATE

Most police officers wear uniforms and a **badge** on their shirts. They carry a gun and **handcuffs**. They use special radios to talk to other police officers. They also use flashlights since they do much of their work at night. Sometimes officers wear special vests to protect them from **bullets**.

← This police officer needs a flashlight to see.

Police officers never know what they might have to do at work. Maybe they will help a lost child find her way home. Maybe they will take care of a car accident. Maybe they will stop a bank robbery!

This police officer helped someone find her way home. →

SPD
POLICE

Police officers have to be prepared for anything. Sometimes they work in teams, so they can help each other. Some officers walk around their community. They check stores and houses to make sure everything is safe.

← Police officers often work together.

Some officers drive around in police cars. They must be able to get around their town or city quickly and easily. When you hear a **siren** and see flashing red lights, you know the police are on their way to help!

Police cars have sirens and flashing red lights. →

NYPD

COMISKEY PARK

Other officers ride horses. Sitting up so high helps the police spot trouble in crowds. Police horses are very well trained. They don't get nervous even on the busiest streets.

← A police officer on horseback helps keep order on the street.

Police officers work with a person at the police station called a dispatcher. When someone calls the station for help, the dispatcher answers the phone. Then she uses her radio to tell officers on the street where the trouble is.

A dispatcher answers a call for help. →

PRIVATE PROPERTY
NO
TRESPASSING

When police officers catch someone breaking the law, they **arrest** the person. They sometimes use handcuffs to help keep the criminal from getting away. Officers prefer not to use their guns. They would rather stop criminals with words than bullets.

← These police officers are arresting someone who broke the law.

Police officers do all kinds of jobs. Some officers direct cars, trucks, and buses in the street. Others visit schools and talk to children about how to stay safe. Some officers are **detectives**. They look for clues to solve crimes.

This police officer works as a detective. →

B.C.S.D.

Some officers work with dogs. Police dogs can sniff out clues and help chase criminals. They are loyal to their officers. When they are not working, police dogs can be very gentle. But it is still important to ask the owners for permission before going near a police dog.

← Police dogs help police officers in many ways.

Police officers are always on the lookout for trouble. They might fly in helicopters or ride on bicycles. They might even race along on snowmobiles! Police officers do whatever it takes to keep their communities safe.

A police officer travels by bicycle at the airport. →

TWA
Bahamasair
POLICE

Glossary

academy (uh-KAD-uh-mee)
An academy is a school that teaches special subjects.

arrest (uh-REST)
To arrest someone means to stop and hold someone by the power of the law.

badge (BAJ)
A badge is a small sign you wear as a member of a profession or club.

bullets (BUL-itz)
Bullets are pieces of metal that are fired from guns.

criminals (KRIM-ih-nuhlz)
Criminals are people who break the law.

detectives (di-TEK-tivz)
Detectives are police officers who look for clues to solve crimes.

handcuffs (HAND-kuhfs)
Handcuffs are metal rings that lock around a criminal's wrists to prevent escape.

siren (SYE-rehn)
A siren is a kind of whistle that makes a loud sound to warn people.

Index

badge, 11
bicycles, 28
community, 4, 15, 28
criminals, 4, 23, 27
detectives, 24
dispatcher, 20
flashlights, 11
gun, 11, 23
handcuffs, 11, 23
helicopters, 28
law, 4, 8, 23
police academy, 8
police cars, 16
police dogs, 27
police horses, 19
radios, 11, 20
snowmobiles, 28
uniforms, 11

To Find Out More

Books

Broekel, Ray. *Police.* Chicago: Childrens Press, 1981.

Flanagan, Alice. *Officer Brown Keeps Neighborhoods Safe.* Danbury, Conn.: Children's Press, 1998.

Russell, Joan Plummer. *Aero and Officer Mike: Police Partners.* Honesdale, Pa.: Boyd's Mill Press, 2001.

Schomp, Virginia. *If You Were a Police Officer.* New York: Benchmark Books, 1998.

Web Sites

Visit our homepage for lots of links about police officers:
http://www.childsworld.com/links.html

Note to Parents, Teachers, and Librarians:
We routinely verify our Web links to make sure they're safe, active sites—so encourage your readers to check them out!

Note to Parents and Educators

Welcome to Wonder Books®! These books provide text at three different levels for beginning readers to practice and strengthen their reading skills. Additionally, the use of nonfiction text provides readers the valuable opportunity to *read to learn*, not just to learn to read.

These leveled readers allow children to choose books at their level of reading confidence and performance. Nonfiction Level One books offer beginning readers simple language, word choice, and sentence structure as well as a word list. Nonfiction Level Two books feature slightly more difficult vocabulary, longer sentences, and longer total text. In the back of each Nonfiction Level Two book are an index and a list of books and Web sites for finding out more information. Nonfiction Level Three books continue to extend word choice and length of text. In the back of each Nonfiction Level Three book are a glossary, an index, and a list of books and Web sites for further research.

State and national standards in reading and language arts emphasize using nonfiction at all levels of reading development. Wonder Books® fill the historical void in nonfiction material for primary grade readers with the additional benefit of a leveled text.

About the Author

Charnan Simon lives in Madison, Wisconsin, with her husband and two daughters. She began her publishing career in the children's book division of Little, Brown and Company, and then became an editor of *Cricket Magazine*. Simon is currently a contributing editor for *Click Magazine* and an author with more than 40 books to her credit. When she is not busy writing, she enjoys reading, gardening, and spending time with her family.